CRISIS AT HOME AND ABROAD:
THE GREAT DEPRESSION, WORLD WAR II, AND BEYOND
*1929-1959*

# TITLE LIST

# CRISIS AT HOME AND ABROAD:
# THE GREAT DEPRESSION, WORLD WAR II, AND BEYOND
## *1929-1959*

BY
**SHEILA NELSON**

**MASON CREST PUBLISHERS**
**PHILADELPHIA**

Mason Crest Publishers Inc.
370 Reed Road
Broomall, Pennsylvania 19008
(866) MCP-BOOK (toll free)

First printing
1 2 3 4 5 6 7 8 9 10

Library of Congress Cataloging-in-Publication Data

Nelson, Sheila.
  Crisis at home and abroad : the Great Depression, World War II, and beyond, 1929–1959 / by Sheila Nelson.
    p. cm. — (How Canada became Canada)
  Includes bibliographical references and index.
  ISBN 1-4222-0007-8    ISBN 1-4222-0000-0 (series)
  1. Canada—History—1914–1945—Juvenile literature. 2. Canada—History—1945—Juvenile literature. I. Title.
  F1034.N37 2006
  971.06—dc22
                        2005012753

Produced by Harding House Publishing Service, Inc.
www.hardinghousepages.com
Interior design by MK Bassett-Harvey.
Cover design by Dianne Hodack.
Printed in Hashemite Kingdom of Jordan.

## CONTENTS

## INTRODUCTION

*by David Bercuson*

Every country's history is distinct, and so is Canada's. Although Canada is often said to be a pale imitation of the United States, it has a unique history that has created a modern North American nation on its own path to democracy and social justice. This series explains how that happened.

Canada's history is rooted in its climate, its geography, and in its separate political development. Virtually all of Canada experiences long, dark, and very cold winters with copious amounts of snowfall. Canada also spans several distinct geographic regions, from the rugged western mountain ranges on the Pacific coast to the forested lowlands of the St. Lawrence River Valley and the Atlantic tidewater region.

Canada's regional divisions were complicated by the British conquest of New France at the end of the Seven Years' War in 1763. Although Britain defeated France, the French were far more numerous in Canada than the British. Britain was thus forced to recognize French Canadian rights to their own language, religion, and culture. That recognition is now enshrined in the Canadian Constitution. It has made Canada a democracy that values group rights alongside individual rights, with official French/English bilingualism as a key part of the Canadian character.

During the American Revolution, Canadians chose to stay British. After the Revolution, they provided refuge to tens of thousands of Americans who, for one reason or another, did not follow George Washington, Benjamin Franklin, or the other founders of the United States who broke with Britain.

Democracy in Canada under the British Crown evolved more slowly than it did in the United States. But in the early nineteenth century, slavery was outlawed in the

British Empire, and as a result, also in Canada. Thus Canada never experienced civil war or government-imposed racial segregation.

From these few, brief examples, it is clear that Canada's history differs considerably from that of the United States. And yet today, Canada is a true North American democracy in its own right. Canadians will profit from a better understanding of how their country was shaped—and Americans may learn much about their own country by studying the story of Canada.

# Halifax Chronicle

"A dependable newspaper"

SCOTIA, WEDNESDAY, OCTOBER 30, 1929

Price Three Cents

16 Pages

Maritime Forecast —
grain whistles fair and cold

# SELLING FRENZY MAKES NEW DRAMA IN MARKET

## ONTARIO VOTERS TODAY, PICK OUT 103 LEGISLATORS

Eight Of 112 Members Already Elected — One Election Deferred

### LIQUOR CONTROL ACT LAUDED BY PREMIER

Liberal Leader Calls For Plebiscite On Liquor Question — Progressives "Bone Dry"

TORONTO, Oct. 30 —

## Crash Takes $1,000,000 From Halifax Traders

### Local Traders Harshly Drubbed In Yesterday's Stock Market Debacle — One Man Drops $75,000 — Another Has Lost $250,000 Since Decline Set In

By JAMES L. McKAY

(Financial Editor of The Halifax Chronicle and The Halifax Daily Star)

Halifax traders are another terrific jolt when prices crashed to new lows in yesterday's wild trading on the New York and Montreal stock Exchanges.

Many traders, unable to carry their holdings any longer threw them over, and accepted whatever gains was offered on the Exchanges at the close.

## MIDDLEWEIGHT KING SAVAGELY MAULS 'WILDCAT'

## FRANTIC SELLING BREAKS RECORDS IN STOCK MARKET

Volume Of Trading Last Week's Record Millions Of Shares

### DAY'S TURNOVER 16,410,000 SHARES

Powerful Interests Come To Halt Debacle — Insurance Companies Advised To Invest

By CLAUDE A.

NEW YORK, Oct. 30 —

## WRITS IN LIBEL SUITS SERVED ON DR. W. D. FORREST

# One

## THE GREAT DEPRESSION

The trading floor of the Toronto Stock Exchange was in chaos. On the morning of October 29, 1929, panicked voices shouted over one another. Here and there, men leaned against the walls, hands over their faces as if trying to shut out the scene. In the street outside, a crowd had gathered, trying to learn the news. A man staggered out the door, clutching his hat in both hands. He looked as though he might weep. "It's gone," he whispered, so quietly only the few closest to him heard. "It's all gone."

## The Wheat Harvests

While the stock market crash of October 1929 was the start of the Great Depression for much of the world, hardships for farmers on the Canadian Prairies had begun several months earlier. In 1928, the wheat crop had been much larger than usual. Since so much wheat was available, prices were very low. Rather than sell the entire crop at such low prices, much of the wheat was stored in grain elevators. Canadians hoped to sell the wheat to Americans or Europeans for higher prices another year, when wheat was scarcer.

The summer of 1929 was dry, and the wheat crop was small that year. When Canadians tried to sell their stored grain, however, they found no one would buy it at higher prices. They soon learned that year's

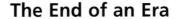

wheat crop in Argentina had been large, and rather than buy more expensive Canadian wheat, many bought the Argentinean crop. The wheat harvest had been large in Europe as well, and Europeans did not need to supplement their own production with Canadian wheat. Canadians were left with overflowing grain elevators and nowhere to sell it. Farmers relying on the sale of their wheat crops to make ends meet could only turn to the government in search of financial aid.

## The End of an Era

In the years after the First World War, the economy boomed. People were racing to buy *stocks* as a way to invest for the future. Many investors even borrowed money so they could buy stocks, since they expected their value to rise. At the beginning of 1929, the stock market looked strong. In September, stocks hit an all-time high.

Then the first signs of trouble began. Throughout the early fall, stocks rose and fell. The market began slipping seriously on October 24, a day that became known as Black Thursday. People panicked, but the next day the market rallied a little. Then on Monday, stocks fell even more, and the next day, Black Tuesday, was even worse than Black Thursday had been. In only a few hours, thousands of people had lost their entire life savings, and many were in debt for the money they had borrowed to buy now-worthless stock.

*Canada's wheatfields dried up.*

Many companies did not survive the stock market crash. Thousands of people were left unemployed as their jobs disappeared in company bankruptcies. The 1920s had been a time of wealth and luxury for many, but that time was over. The widespread hardships of the Great Depression had only just started.

***Stocks*** *are shares of ownership in a company held by investors.*

*Out-of-work men during the Great Depression in Canada*

## R. B. Bennett

When the Great Depression hit Canada in 1929, William Lyon Mackenzie King and the Liberal Party had been in power for most of the previous seven years. Now, thousands lined up in unemployment lines looking for work. Charities handed out food to the starving, but there was never enough to go around. When the time came for a general election in 1930, Canadians looked to see who would help them out of their desperate situation.

Richard Bedford Bennett, a member of the Conservative Party, announced that if elected, he and his government would end the Great Depression and the unemployment that had arrived with it, or "perish in the attempt." Prime Minister King, on the other hand, believed the federal govern-

*R. B. Bennett with his sister Mildred, who acted as his hostess.*

ment should not have to provide assistance for unemployed people. He thought the provinces and cities should take care of their own people. At one point during the election campaign, King announced that he would not give "a five-cent piece" to any province with a Conservative government. This statement did not go over well with Conservatives around the country.

With R. B. Bennett promising to end Canada's unemployment problems and King claiming relief efforts were not a federal issue, the election took place on July 28, 1930. When the results were in, Canadians had chosen Bennett and the Conservatives to lead the country.

One of the first things Bennett did as prime minister was raise the *tariffs* on imported goods. He hoped to protect Canadian manufacturers and producers from competition from foreign markets, but many other countries had also reacted to the Depression by establishing similar tariffs. As a result, Canadian export products suffered as the countries of the world retreated protectively behind their borders.

Bennett increased *relief spending* and set up work camps for unemployed men. These camps were intended to decrease unemployment, giving young men something to do. Most work camps were in rural areas and very rustic. The men lived in rough shacks and worked six and a half days a week doing manual labor. In return, they received a place to sleep, meals, and twenty cents a day. This wage was very low, and eventually, the men got tired of it. They wanted to have normal lives, to get married and start families, but the only jobs available to them were in the work camps.

When the Depression began, everyone had hoped it would be over soon. Bennett had great hopes that he would be able to help bring Canada out of the economic crisis, but the

*Tariffs* are taxes levied on imported, and sometimes exported, goods.

*Relief spending* is providing payments to individuals in need of assistance to pay for their living expenses.

*Prime Minister King in his library*

13

# Letters to Bennett

During the Great Depression, thousands of Canadians wrote letters to Prime Minister Bennett, asking him for food, clothing, or money. Parents wrote desperately looking for money to buy food for their children. One woman wrote asking for a pair of long underwear for her husband. A little boy wrote asking for a red wagon. Bennett did what he could for the Canadian people, answering many letters personally and adding his own money to the envelopes. In spite of the increasing bitterness of Canadians toward him, Bennett was an extremely generous man who sincerely cared about people.

worldwide Depression was too much for him. Bennett did not get along with others easily; he was arrogant and abrasive, and Canadians soon grew to resent him. The Great Depression deepened and poverty increased. For millions, there was no hope in sight. Bennett had been taught hard work was the only way to success and had, in fact, become a millionaire through his own business interests. When Bennett told Canadians during the worst years of the Depression that "One of the greatest assets any man or woman can have on entering life's struggle is poverty," many reacted badly. Bennett had not ended unemployment; in fact, more than a quarter of all Canadians were unemployed. Two million people lived on relief handouts, out of a population of ten million.

In the West, conditions were the worst. After the bumper crop of 1928, a drought began that lasted for nearly a decade. The soil was so dry that by the early 1930s it began to blow away. Soon huge dust storms raced across the Canadian prairies and the American plains, dumping tons of dirt on towns and cities as they passed. The prairie farmers had experienced dust storms before, but they had never been so widespread and so long lasting.

On the heels of the dust storms came a plague of grasshoppers in 1932. The grasshoppers ate everything they could find—grass, trees, and the clothes hanging out to dry. People could not walk outside without crushing dozens of grasshoppers underfoot.

*The **international gold standard** was the monetary system in which the economy was based on the fixed weight of gold.*

## Bennett's Popularity Fades

As the Depression years wore on, Canadians became completely frustrated with Prime Minister Bennett. He had not only failed to improve Depression conditions, but conditions had gotten worse since he had taken office. This was not Bennett's fault exactly, since the Great Depression involved many conditions beyond his control, such as high tariffs imposed by countries around the world, the collapse of the *international gold standard*, and the droughts on the prairies.

Canadians began to call the old broken-down cars that had to be pulled by a team of horses "Bennett buggies." Newspapers, used to cover homeless men on park benches, were called "Bennett blankets." Bennett's name was linked bitterly with anything that spoke of Depression-era poverty and want.

By 1935, the men in the work camps had had enough. They felt like slaves, unable to come and go as they pleased, unable to marry and start families, unable even to save any money

*The On-to-Ottawa Trek*

15

for the future. They called themselves the "Royal Twenty-Centers" because of the twenty cents they earned each day, and the name became increasingly bitter.

In the spring of 1935, they went on strike. The strike began in British Columbia, led by Arthur Evans, a longtime *union activist*. Determined to take their complaints directly to Bennett in Ottawa, over a thousand men

*Hundreds of men piled on boxcars to Ottawa.*

piled into boxcars to ride the rails east to Ottawa.

News of the "On-to-Ottawa Trek" raced across Canada ahead of the strikers. At each stop along the way, the men found people waiting for the train, offering them food, encouragement, and a place to stay. Men from other work camps hurried down to the railway to join the strike and the On-to-Ottawa Trek.

Bennett was nervous. He did not want nearly two thousand striking workers descending on Ottawa. He gave orders for Royal Canadian Mounted Police (RCMP) to stop the trek at Regina, Saskatchewan. The strikers would not be allowed to get back on the trains. To make sure that the men would not disperse to cause more trouble or find other ways to Ottawa, the RCMP sealed all exits to the city. The strikers would be kept in Regina until they agreed to go willingly to a special work camp created in a nearby town specifically to contain the belligerent young men.

Finally, Bennett agreed to allow a delegation to travel to Ottawa and meet with him. The meeting was not a success. Bennett accused the men of being communists and thieves; Arthur Evans retorted that Bennett was a liar.

The delegation returned to Regina discouraged. Nothing had been accomplished.

Violence in Regina

*A **union activist** is someone who takes vigorous, sometimes aggressive action in favor of labor unions.*

The government would not agree to improve the conditions at the work camps and pay the workers a higher wage, and the workers would not agree to give up their fight and be herded into the camp.

For days, nothing happened. Then, on the evening of July 1, a small group of strikers held a public meeting in Regina's Market Square. No sooner had the meeting begun than several squads of RCMP officers leapt out and began trying to round up people and put them under arrest. The policemen had clubs, guns, and tear gas grenades, but the strikers fought back. Soon, over a hundred men had been arrested, including Evans and the other strike leaders. Dozens had been injured, and one plainclothes policeman had been killed.

*Poster supporting the Trekkers*

*William Lyon Mackenzie King*

After the riot, the strike leaders were forced to remain in prison while awaiting trial, but the other men were allowed to return home. The Saskatchewan government, eager to regain peace in the province, paid for their trips home, and they rode passenger trains with as much food as they needed. Bennett believed he had won, since he had prevented the strikers from continuing on to Ottawa and had not given in to their demands for higher wages and better conditions in the camps. The strikers had at least won a minor victory, however, since they had returned home in style instead of being forced into the special work camp.

The real impact of the On-to-Ottawa Trek came as the October general election approached. The strike had caught the imagination and sympathy of Canadians, and Bennett's popularity fell even lower. William Lyon Mackenzie King campaigned against Bennett, running with the slogan "King or Chaos!" Canadians had had enough chaos under Bennett, and they were more than willing to give King and the Liberals another chance. The Liberals swept the election, bringing King back into power.

The worst of the Depression was over by 1935, fortunately for King. The new prime minister shut down the work camps and instituted the National Employment Commission to look into the best ways to deal with unemployment. The commission presented a report recommending an unemployment insurance program, which the King government eventually put into place. Bennett had tried to introduce similar reforms earlier, but Canadians had not trusted his sudden change of heart, and the reform programs fell through.

Although conditions improved in Canada by the second half of the 1930s, the Great Depression would not end until the beginning of World War II. The war years would bring increased economic growth, but at the price of millions of lives lost, thousands of them Canadian.

*Canadian troops disembarking*

# Two

## CANADA JOINS THE WAR

In the early morning hours of September 1, 1939, the inhabitants of the little Polish town of Wielun slept peacefully in their beds, unaware of the German bombers headed toward them. At 4:40 A.M., the bombs began to fall, striking homes and a hospital, killing 1,200 people. The Germans attacked in the *blitzkrieg* style, quickly and without warning, like lightning striking out of a clear sky. Seventy-five percent of the town was destroyed in the surprise attack.

Adolph Hitler, Germany's dictator, did not expect the world to react to his invasion of Poland. After all, he had **annexed** both Austria and Czechoslovakia, and no one had made any move to stop him. Britain had made a treaty to protect Poland if it were to be attacked, but Hitler did not expect Britain to follow through on its promise.

Hitler wanted to rule the world, and to remove those he believed unfit to live in the same world as his blond-haired, blue-eyed master **Aryan** race. The Jews bore the brunt of

*Annexed means added.*

*In Nazi ideology, the Aryan race refers to a Caucasian person of non-Semitic descent regarded as racially superior.*

Hitler's hatred—six million of them would be massacred in death camps before the war ended—but gypsies, homosexuals, and the physically and mentally disabled were also outside Hitler's plan for the world.

Hours after the attack, the Polish government sent an emergency message to the governments of Britain and France, begging for their immediate help. Two days later, both Britain and France declared war on Germany.

*The Royal Canadian Air Force*

## Canada at War

When World War I had begun in 1914, Canada had automatically been at war as soon as Britain declared war. Since then, Canada had gained a much greater independence from Britain. After Britain and France declared war on Germany on September 3, the Canadian Parliament met to discuss the part Canada should play in the international crisis. All but three *MPs* voted to go to war. A week later, on September 10, Canada entered the war. Prime Minister King waited a week to announce Canada's declaration of war only to emphasize Canada's independence from Britain.

During the first months of the war, Canada, along with Britain and France, braced for fighting, but very little happened. In the Atlantic, German U-boat submarines tried to sink British ships and North American ships carrying supplies to Britain. The Canadian navy worked with the British navy to help protect the supply convoys.

The relative peace of the first few months of war made many people believe the war would soon be over. Canada readied its military and sent troops to Britain, but the government did not see the need to try and increase enlistment numbers greatly. Prime Minister King offered to build training facilities for pilots in Canada. The British Commonwealth Air Training Plan would allow pilots from Britain, Canada, Australia, and New Zealand to train in Canada, safe from the fighting in Europe. King hoped the plan would act as Canada's main contribution to the war effort.

In May of 1940, the *Allies*' hopes for a quick end to the war were shattered when Germany launched a sudden assault against France. The border between France and Germany had

*MPs* are Members of Parliament.

*The **Allies** were a military alliance composed of France, Great Britain, Russia, and the United States.*

*Canadian pilot*

been well fortified with France's Maginot Line, and the French government was confident it could hold off a German attack in this area. Germany did not waste its troops on the Maginot Line, however, and chose instead to go around the line. The attack came through the neutral countries of Belgium and the Netherlands and through the Ardennes Forest, which the Allies had believed was impassible. France's defenses were much weaker along these northern borders. Germany attacked fiercely, taking the Allies by surprise. Britain quickly evacuated as many of its soldiers as possible. By the end of June, the Germans had pushed all the way across the north of France. On June 25, France surrendered and became an occupied country.

*German U-boat*

## The Battle of Britain

After France fell, Germany turned its eyes toward Britain. Since Great Britain was an island, Germany could not simply march its troops across the border to attack; the assault needed to come by air or water. Throughout the war, German U-boats prowled the Atlantic, sinking Allied naval and merchant ships, but never landed troops on British soil. The air war began in July of 1940 and continued through May of 1941. During this time, the German *Luftwaffe*—air force—kept up a constant aerial bombardment of Britain. The initial bombing raids were aimed at destroying the Royal Air Force (RAF), so they targeted airfields and radar stations. If the RAF were crushed, Germany would have a much better chance at succeeding in an invasion.

The RAF was suffering under the steady barrage of bombings and was close to the point of collapse, but then, in late August, a German pilot missed his target and accidentally dropped his bomb on London. In retaliation, the RAF launched a bombing attack against Berlin, in Germany. Angry at this attack, Hitler ordered the Luftwaffe to break off their RAF-targeted raids and focus on destroying London.

For the next two months, London and other British cities faced day and night bombardment. Since the focus was no longer on RAF targets, the pilots could regroup and were better able to fight off the attackers. Tirelessly, the RAF patrolled the skies, battling the

*The Battle of Britain*

*The **Commonwealth** refers to the Commonwealth of Nations, an association consisting of Britain and sovereign states that were formerly British colonies or are ruled by Britain.*

Luftwaffe in the air. Many Canadians fought with them, in the air or on the ground, as did pilots from other **Commonwealth** countries and those who had fled to Britain from occupied European countries.

Eventually, the Luftwaffe could no longer keep up the intensity of constant bombing raids. Every day, they lost more planes. They were fighting over enemy territory, far from their own airfields and refueling stations. The German commanders also suffered from a lack of information about the effects their attacks were having. They did not know if or how well they were succeeding in crushing the spirit of the British people.

The British people called the prolonged attack the Blitz, short for blitzkrieg, although the bombardment was not a true "lightning war." At night, the cities were in blackout, with thick curtains keeping even a sliver of light from shining through the windows. Any light at all could give the German bombers a target. Whenever the air-raid siren sounded, telling people the enemy had been sighted in the sky, everyone fled

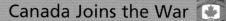

to the air-raid shelters until the all-clear siren wailed its distinctive note. Most children were sent to stay in the country, or overseas to Canada, to protect them from the bombings in the city. The cities were dangerous places during the Blitz; thousands were left homeless and thousands more killed over the months of bombardment.

Hitler expected British society to fall apart. He waited for the people to turn on each other in their fear and panic, but it did not happen. Instead, the people took strength from banding together to help each other survive. They battled the flames ignited by German fire bombs. They huddled inside their dark houses and listened to the encouraging and inspiring words of their prime minister, Winston Churchill, on the radio.

27

"The British nation and the British Empire finding themselves alone, stood undismayed against disaster," came Churchill's instantly recognizable voice.

No one flinched or wavered; nay, some who formerly thought of peace, now think only of war. Our people are united and resolved, as they have never been before. Death and ruin have become small things compared with the shame of defeat or failure in duty. We cannot tell what lies ahead. It may be that even greater ordeals lie before us. We shall face whatever is coming to us.

The Battle of Britain continued for months, although the worst of it was over by the end of October 1940. In May of 1941,

*Winston Churchill*

*London's St. Paul's Cathedral during the Blitz*

Germany stopped its bombing raids to focus on an invasion of the Soviet Union, its former ally.

## The Defense of Hong Kong

While Adolph Hitler aggressively expanded Germany's borders in Europe, Japan began to make similar aggressive moves in Asia. One of the first major battles of the Second World War that involved Canada took place on the island of Hong Kong, then a British colony. In November of 1941, Canada sent nearly two thousand soldiers to Hong Kong to help Britain protect the colony from the increasing Japanese threat. On the morning of December 8, Japanese forces attacked Hong Kong, only hours after their attack on the American naval base at Pearl Harbor in Hawaii. The Canadian soldiers on the island were inexperienced fighters and not

*Smoke from Japanese bombs dropped on Hong Kong*

completely trained. All their equipment had not yet arrived from Canada, and they were not prepared to fight 50,000 well-trained Japanese soldiers.

Despite their inexperience, the Canadian soldiers fought bravely, together with British forces, holding off the Japanese for seventeen days. On December 25, the British governor of Hong Kong surrendered to the Japanese. Over five hundred Canadian soldiers had been killed by this point; the rest were taken prisoner and spent the remainder of the war in the Japanese prison camps.

## Dieppe

With the end of the Battle of Britain in the spring of 1941, the Allies began to work out a plan to liberate France from German occupation. Allied commanders decided to launch a test raid against the French town of Dieppe. The Allied soldiers would land on the beach and capture the town, holding it for a short time. The purpose of the raid was to see if such an attack would be possible on a larger scale and to gather intelligence from German prisoners and from examining German equipment on the ground. The Allies intended to watch closely the German response to such a raid so they could better predict future actions.

Of the 6,100 men involved, 5,000 were Canadians. The exact details of the plan were complicated and unrealistic. The first wave of Canadian soldiers was to capture the beach, scale the cliffs, and take out the German defenses before the main attack came half an hour later.

*Canadian troops at Dieppe before the battle*

*Canadian troops during battle*

The raid failed completely. Many of the soldiers had never been in battle before and were not sufficiently trained to deal with the attack's intricate details. Some men were dropped off in the wrong places, spreading the attack too thinly. The pebbly beaches clogged the treads of the tanks intended to provide crucial defenses and artillery support, stalling them at the water's edge. Men fell in a rain of German machine-gun fire, killed instantly or drowned in the incoming tide.

The battle lasted nine hours. When it was over, and those who could retreat had done so, over nine hundred Canadians were dead and nearly two thousand had been cap-tured, to be taken to German prison camps; thousands had been injured.

Although the raid itself was a disaster and accomplished none of its goals, the Allies did learn valuable lessons from it for the future. Most important, they learned

*Canadian soldiers*

# The Liberation of the Netherlands

On May 5, 1945, two days before Germany surrendered completely, the Germans surrendered the Netherlands. For months, Canadian forces had fought to push the Germans out of the Netherlands. The campaign cost more than 7,600 Canadian lives. After the war, the Dutch honored the Canadian troops for their effort on behalf of their country. A bond of friendship born of Canadian sacrifice and Dutch appreciation arose between the Netherlands and Canada. Even today, the Canadian war heroes of World War II are given special recognition in the Netherlands.

what not to do in an attack—not to send inexperienced troops to attack heavily fortified, cliff-ringed beaches, for example.

## Freeing France

In 1944, the Allies were finally ready to launch a major invasion against German-occupied France. The invasion of Normandy was the largest attack ever launched across water. The attack began on June 6, D-Day. The Allies did not try to depend heavily on stealth and surprise. They had done this at Dieppe, and it had backfired when the Germans discovered the attack before the Allies arrived. For days before the D-Day attack, airplanes and ships bombarded the

*Celebrating the liberation of the Netherlands*

*Conscription* is the man-datory enrollment of citizens for a specified period of service, usually in the armed forces.

French coastline in a number of areas. On the night before the main assault, the bombers concentrated on the landing sites on the Normandy beaches.

In the early morning of June 6, 1944, the invasion of Normandy began. Tens of thousands of men landed on the

*Canadian troops disembarking on D-Day*

beaches from ships in the English Channel. More soldiers parachuted in from airplanes and attacked the Germans from behind their lines of defense. Allied soldiers landed simultaneously on five different beaches in one area of the northern French coastline.

The Canadian Third Division was assigned the capture of Juno Beach, the second most heavily fortified of the landing sites. Although their casualty rate was high, as was that of the other invasion forces, the Canadian troops were able to push through the German defenses. By the end of the day, the Canadians had penetrated farther into France than had any of the other attacking forces.

D-Day was just the beginning of the Battle of Normandy. For months, the Allies fought to capture northern France. In August, more Allied troops attacked the south of France from the Mediterranean and fought their way north. Late in August, the Allies neared Paris. The French within the city refused to fight for the Germans, and many aided the Allies by barricading streets and taking up arms against the German occupiers. On August 25, the German general in charge of the city surrendered, turning Paris over to the Allies despite the fact that Hitler had ordered the city be destroyed rather than captured. The next day, Allied troops marched victoriously into Paris, and people danced joyously in the streets.

In the fall of 1944, the Allies moved quickly across France and into Belgium, pushing the German forces back in front of them. Canadian forces worked to liberate the Netherlands, driving the Germans still further back throughout late 1944 and early 1945. By the spring of 1945, the Allies had entered Germany: the Canadians, British, French, and Americans from the east and the Soviets from the west.

Seeing his empire crumble around him, Hitler committed suicide on April 30 in his bunker under Berlin. On May 7, Germany surrendered unconditionally to the Allies. The war in Europe was over.

In the Pacific, the war lasted nearly four months longer, ending in September after the United States dropped two atomic bombs on Japanese cities.

Although most of the fighting of the Second World War had taken place far from Canada, Canadians at home faced the effects of the war. Issues such as *conscription*, controversial during World War I, were debated again. Canadians examined their part in the war effort as the fighting overseas continued. German U-boats crept into Canadian harbors, bringing the war to Canada in a way people had not expected.

The inhabitants of peaceful Gaspé Peninsula assumed they were safe from the violence of World War II.

# *Three*
## THE HOMEFRONT

On a May night in 1942, Canadians slept, believing themselves safe from the distant war. A sudden explosion in the Gulf of St. Lawrence shook the houses in little fishing villages along the northeastern shore of Québec's Gaspé Peninsula. People rushed to see what had happened, but all that was visible were some lights at sea that quickly disappeared. In the morning, frightened men drifted ashore in lifeboats, telling of an underwater attack that had come out of nowhere.

Soon, word spread across Canada. The unthinkable had happened. German U-boat submarines were in Canadian harbors, attacking Canadian ships. No longer could Canadians feel safely distant from the fighting overseas.

## U-Boats in Canada

In the 1920s, one Canadian politician had summed up the Canadian position by stating that they "lived in a fireproof house, far from inflammable materials." People had believed for years that Canada was safe from upheaval in Europe and sufficiently isolated to be protected from the threat of attacks. With the beginnings of the U-boat attacks in 1942, Canadians could no longer embrace that comfortable sentiment. For the next two years, Canadian ships faced the constant threat of attack by German submarines, whether they were in the middle of the Atlantic Ocean on the way to bring supplies to Britain or simply traveling along the St. Lawrence River in the heart of Canada. The German U-boats targeted naval and civilian boats alike.

During the summer of 1942, submarines entered the St. Lawrence River and sank twenty-three ships. In response, Prime Minister King closed the river to shipping vessels.

On October 14, 1942, the S.S. *Caribou*, a passenger ferry, was on the way from Nova Scotia to Newfoundland with nearly three hundred people on board. At three-thirty in the morning, a U-boat attacked, blowing a hole in the side of the *Caribou* so large the ship sank within five minutes. A *corvette* had been assigned to accompany the *Caribou*, because of a report that a U-boat had been spotted in the area, but the warship was unable to locate the submarine

after the attack. Over a hundred people from the *Caribou* died, including ten of the eleven children on board.

The constant submarine threat was terrifying. U-boats traveling under the water were hard to detect, although developments in radar technology helped. British Prime Minister Winston Churchill later admitted he had found the U-boats the most frightening aspect of the war.

*A **corvette** is an armed naval escort vehicle.*

*The S.S. Caribou in dock before its destruction*

*A Canadian corvette*

## The Second Conscription Crisis

At the beginning of the war, when little appeared to be happening in most of Europe, Canadians started to believe the matter would be resolved quickly. The Canadian military prepared for war and accepted new recruits, but most believed conscription would not be necessary. During World War I, Canada had begun an unpopular conscription at the very end of the war, but in the early years of this war, such a policy did not appear to be needed.

In March of 1940, William Lyon Mackenzie King called a general election. People usually preferred government stability during war years, and Canadians were not very interested in electing a new prime minister.

To solidify that support, Prime Minister King promised not to introduce a conscription policy. King was reelected with the overwhelming support of the Canadian people.

Shortly after the election, Germany invaded and conquered France, and the war entered a more critical phase. In June, King passed the National Resources Mobilization Act (NRMA). Under the act, all eligible Canadian men over sixteen years of age were required to register with the government. In April of 1941, Canada began drafting young men under the NRMA to help protect Canada at home. King hoped this action would satisfy those Canadians who wanted a conscription policy without angering those who did not. It did neither, in fact, leaving both sides discontented. Eventually, over 60,000 men were drafted to protect Canada. The NRMA men had so little to do that Canadians nicknamed them "Zombies."

When the war expanded to include Japan, Prime Minister King realized he might need more men to help fight the war. Canada was contributing food and supplies to the war effort, and had instituted the British Commonwealth Air Training Plan to train pilots, but the Allies needed soldiers to win the war.

In April of 1942, King held a national *plebiscite* to determine the position of

*Royal Canadian Air Force crew*

Canadians on conscription. In his speech describing the need to release the government from its pledge not to institute conscription, King told Canadians that allowing him to simply have the option of considering conscription sometime in the future would make the Canadian war effort look better to the rest of the world. When Canadians voted, they voted not on whether to institute conscription but on whether to consider conscription as a possibility. The vote was close, but 64 percent voted yes, and King was free to seriously consider

*A **plebiscite** is a vote by an entire electorate to decide a question of importance.*

43

*Canadian soldiers*

conscription. Seventy-three percent of those voting no were from Québec.

Before beginning a conscription policy, King tried to meet the need for soldiers by other means. He brought in a new minister of defense to increase enlistment numbers, but still not enough men volunteered for service.

Prime Minister King knew the country was still divided on the issue of conscription, and he wanted to please as many people as possible. He put the decision off as

44

long as he could, but the need for more soldiers was becoming desperate, especially with the intensive fighting in France after the invasion of Normandy. Finally, he came up with an idea. Instead of drafting more people, he would draft the Zombies. These men had already been conscripted to defend Canada.

Most Canadians accepted this compromise, but the Zombies were not pleased. One group went on strike rather than willingly board ships to travel overseas. Eventually, 13,000 Zombies left Canada, although the war ended before most of them reached the battlefield. Of the 2,500 who did go into battle, 69 were killed.

*Canadian marines*

## Japanese Internment Camps

With the beginning of war with Japan in December of 1941, Canadians turned suspicious eyes on the thousands of Japanese immigrants living within their borders. Almost immediately, Canada began relocating everyone of Japanese descent who lived along the Pacific Coast. Canadians feared these Japanese Canadians would suddenly rise up against Canada and fight to take the country from within on behalf of Japan.

Over 22,000 Japanese Canadians were sent to relocation centers in Canada. Most of the men were forced to work on road-building projects or on farms, while the women and children were transported to several towns deep in the wilderness of British Columbia. These families lost everything overnight, as they were roused from their

*A Japanese internment camp in British Columbia*

sleep and given only a few hours to prepare for relocation. They could bring only as much as they could carry. The Canadian government took control of the property and businesses left behind, usually selling the belongings at public auction. The Japanese did not resist being uprooted and sent to remote internment camps. Their culture had taught them to accept what could not be helped.

In the camps, the Japanese faced terrible poverty and primitive conditions. They were not kept in with barbed wire fences, but they were so far from developed towns that they could not think of leaving. The camps had no electricity or running water, and the Canadian government provided residents with very little food. Hearing of the internment camps, people in Japan sent

# NOTICE TO ALL JAPANESE PERSONS AND PERSONS OF JAPANESE RACIAL ORIGIN

TAKE NOTICE that under Orders Nos. 21, 22, 23 and 24 of the British Columbia Security Commission, the following areas were made prohibited areas to all persons of the Japanese race:—

LULU ISLAND
   (including Steveston)
SEA ISLAND
EBURNE
MARPOLE
DISTRICT OF
   QUEENSBOROUGH
CITY OF
   NEW WESTMINSTER

SAPPERTON
BURQUITLAM
PORT MOODY
IOCO
PORT COQUITLAM
MAILLARDVILLE
FRASER MILLS

AND FURTHER TAKE NOTICE that any person of the Japanese race found within any of the said prohibited areas without a written permit from the British Columbia Security Commission or the Royal Canadian Mounted Police shall be liable to the penalties provided under Order in Council P.C. 1665.

AUSTIN C. TAYLOR,

Chairman,

British Columbia Security Commission

*Notice to all Japanese persons*

food through the Red Cross to be distributed to the Japanese Canadians.

After the war, Canada waited another four years before allowing the Japanese to return to the West Coast. Even then, they faced intensive interviews to determine whether they would truly be loyal to Canada. Those who refused to be questioned, or who officials determined to be a risk, were deported to Japan. Over four thousand were eventually forced out of Canada, including many who did not even speak Japanese, having lived their whole lives in Canada. Those who stayed in Canada had to rebuild their lives com-

*One of the Japanese families interred in Canada during World War II*

# Racism in Canada

The Japanese were not the only group who faced persecution in Canada during the war. When Jews fleeing Nazi Germany tried to enter Canada, the government blocked them. Prime Minister King did not want to allow Jews into Canada because he claimed their presence would cause unrest. While other countries accepted tens of thousands of Jewish immigrants, Canada let in less than five thousand.

pletely. Many had been prosperous businesspeople before the war, but now they had nothing.

In 1988, the Canadian government finally issued a formal apology to the Japanese. Those who had been imprisoned during the war could file a claim and receive a compensation of $21,000 each.

With the war over, the soldiers began to return home, and life got back to normal—although the world was changed com-

pletely. The League of Nations, which had seemed like such a good idea after the First World War, had failed to prevent another war. Clearly, an international body like the League of Nations was needed, but it had to have an improved structure and the power to enforce its decisions. In the years after World War II, the countries of the world came together to try to set in place laws and policies that would keep such a widespread conflict from ever happening again.

*Flags of the UN Security Force*

# Four
## UNITING THE WORLD

*We the Peoples of the United Nations determined to save succeeding generations from the scourge of war, which twice in our lifetime has brought untold sorrow to mankind. . . .*

So begins the charter of the United Nations, signed by fifty-one former Allied powers in San Francisco on June 26, 1945. The war with Germany had ended, but the war with Japan would continue for another month and a half. The world was sick of war, and the people wanted peace.

## The United Nations

The Allied nations had begun using the term "United Nations" to describe themselves earlier in the war. The phrase had been chosen by U.S. president Franklin D. Roosevelt and taken up by British prime minister Winston Churchill. When the representatives from fifty-one countries met to form an organization to prevent further wars and uphold the rights and freedoms of humanity, the term was chosen as a name for the new group.

All the original members of the United Nations had been at war with the *Axis* powers during World War II, although

*During World War II, the **Axis** was a military and political alliance between Germany, Italy, and later, Japan.*

*The first assembly of the League of Nations*

more countries quickly joined in the years after the war. At the center of the UN structure is the Security Council, composed of five permanent members—Britain, China, France, the Soviet Union, and the United States. Other members are elected to the Security Council on a rotating basis. The Security Council investigates disputes between nations and works toward peace. Each of the permanent members has veto power during a vote, meaning agreements have to be unanimous between the five countries. The old League of Nations had required complete agreement between all its members before any resolution could be passed, just one of the reasons it failed to be effective.

One of the main reasons for the creation of the United Nations was the upholding of human rights and the prevention of such atrocities as had taken place in the German death camps. The UN created a Human Rights Division and assigned to it the task of drafting a Universal Declaration of Human Rights, intended to guide the actions of UN member countries. John Humphrey, a Canadian from a small town in New Brunswick, served as the first director of the Human Rights Division. Humphrey was a lawyer and had been teaching law at McGill University in Montréal when he was ap-

pointed as director of the UN's Human Rights Division.

Humphrey cared passionately about the rights of all people. He believed human beings should be treated with respect and dignity, no matter their age, gender, race, religion, or political beliefs. Working with a committee, which included the former American first lady Eleanor Roosevelt,

*Eleanor Roosevelt*

# The Preamble of the
# Universal Declaration of Human Rights

Whereas recognition of the inherent dignity and of the equal and inalienable rights of all members of the human family is the foundation of freedom, justice and peace in the world,

Whereas disregard and contempt for human rights have resulted in barbarous acts which have outraged the conscience of mankind, and the advent of a world in which human beings shall enjoy freedom of speech and belief and freedom from fear and want has been proclaimed as the highest aspiration of the common people,

Whereas it is essential, if man is not to be compelled to have recourse, as a last resort, to rebellion against tyranny and oppression, that human rights should be protected by the rule of law,

Whereas it is essential to promote the development of friendly relations between nations,

Whereas the peoples of the United Nations have in the Charter reaffirmed their faith in fundamental human rights, in the dignity and worth of the human person and in the equal rights of men and women and have determined to promote social progress and better standards of life in larger freedom,

Whereas Member States have pledged themselves to achieve, in co-operation with the United Nations, the promotion of universal respect for and observance of human rights and fundamental freedoms,

Whereas a common understanding of these rights and freedoms is of the greatest importance for the full realization of this pledge,

Now, Therefore THE GENERAL ASSEMBLY proclaims THIS UNIVERSAL DECLARATION OF HUMAN RIGHTS as a common standard of achievement for all peoples and all nations, to the end that every individual and every organ of society, keeping this Declaration constantly in mind, shall strive by teaching and education to promote respect for these rights and freedoms and by progressive measures, national and international, to secure their universal and effective recognition and observance, both among the peoples of Member States themselves and among the peoples of territories under their jurisdiction.

Humphrey wrote the first draft of the Universal Declaration of Human Rights. On December 10, 1948, the United Nations adopted the declaration, and since that time it has been used as a basis for the constitutions of many countries, and for Canada's Charter of Rights and Freedoms, adopted in 1982.

The first of the declaration's thirty articles reads, "All human beings are born free and equal in dignity and rights. They are endowed with reason and conscience and should act towards one another in a spirit of brotherhood." This statement is the foundation for the remainder of the articles, which include such things as prohibitions against slavery and torture, the right to freedom of thought and freedom of speech, the right to equal pay for equal work, and the right to an education.

*Communism is the political system in which all property and wealth are controlled by a single totalitarian party.*

## The North Atlantic Treaty Organisation

The Soviet Union is one of the permanent members of the UN's Security Council, but many Western countries feared the spread of Soviet *communism*. After the war, much of Eastern Europe was reorganized with communist governments, and many leaders of other nations worried an attack on democratic countries could soon occur. To protect themselves in the case of such an attack, the countries of Western Europe and North America came together to form NATO, the North Atlantic Treaty Organisation. Twelve countries, including Canada, formed the original NATO members and signed the North Atlantic Treaty on April 4, 1949.

*Louis St. Laurent became prime minister in 1948.*

The North Atlantic Treaty states that any attack against a NATO member will be considered an attack against all member countries. The treaty agrees to seek peaceful solutions to

55

# Original NATO Members

Belgium

Canada

Denmark

France

Iceland

Italy

Luxembourg

Netherlands

Norway

Portugal

United Kingdom

United States

disputes and to uphold the charter of the United Nations, but it also claims the right given in that same charter to defend themselves against aggression if necessary.

In 1948, William Lyon Mackenzie King had stepped down as prime minister and been replaced with Louis St. Laurent, a quiet, dignified man who was nicknamed "Uncle Louis" by the media because of the affection the Canadian people felt for him. St. Laurent was instrumental in bringing Canada into NATO. Some were concerned that by joining NATO Canada was becoming a puppet of the United States, but St. Laurent felt strongly that Canada needed to take its place as a "middle power," an intermediary between the superpowers.

*A **referendum** is a vote by an entire electorate on a specific question or questions put to it by a government body.*

# Newfoundland and Labrador Join Canada

For centuries, the island of Newfoundland had existed as either a British colony or an independent nation. In 1934, at the height of the Great Depression, Newfoundland had given up its self-governing status and returned power to Britain because it could not produce enough money to keep itself going.

The Second World War had devastated Britain while leaving Canada quite wealthy. After the war, Britain encouraged many of its colonies to become independent. When Newfoundland politicians decided to hold a **referendum** to determine the island's future, they at first intended to offer the people a choice between returning to independent rule and remaining under Britain's control. Britain, however, requested the referendum offer a third choice—joining Canada's Confederation.

*Battle Harbor, one of the Newfoundland communities that were relocated*

Joey Smallwood, a Newfoundland politician and journalist, worked hard to promote the idea of confederation. He printed a newspaper called *The Confederate* to inform Newfoundlanders about the benefits of joining Canada. Smallwood was convinced Confederation would increase Newfoundland's prosperity.

The referendum was held on June 3, 1948, but the results did not overwhelmingly favor any of the options. A slight

*A Newfoundland community church*

majority (44.6 percent) favored regaining independence, while nearly as many (41.1 percent) supported joining Canada. Only a few (14.3 percent) voted to continue as a British colony. A second referendum was held on July 22 and this time offered only a choice between independence and joining Canada. Newfoundlanders voted 52 to 48 percent to join Canada, still a close vote but enough for Joey Smallwood to proclaim a victory for confederation.

*Newfoundland fishing community*

On March 31, 1949, Newfoundland and the northern mainland region of Labrador joined Canada as the province of Newfoundland and Labrador, Canada's tenth province. With the addition of Newfoundland and Labrador, the geo-graphic shape of Canada as we know it today was complete.

Joey Smallwood became the first premier of Newfoundland and Labrador; he served in that office for over twenty-two years. He was extremely popular in the province, although he also instituted the controversial practice of resettlement.

## Newfoundland's Resettlement

Thousands of Newfoundlanders lived in tiny outport communities, fishing villages consisting of only a few houses clinging to remote rocky coasts or small islands. Confederation brought an intensive road-building program to Newfoundland, but these roads could not reach many of these remote areas. Nobody could afford to build roads to every community—many of which were on islands—or to string telephone and electrical lines to serve the many far-flung towns. In the early 1950s, Smallwood began a resettlement program.

Under the program, people were offered incentives to move out of the tiny outports and into slightly larger communities. Smallwood claimed he would "drag Newfoundlanders kicking and screaming into the twentieth century" if necessary.

At least 250 outports became ghost towns as thousands of people took up Smallwood's offer. Some towns disappeared completely as families levered their houses off the rocky ground and floated them across the bay to the main island of Newfoundland. Some people left willingly, while others were pressured to leave by their neighbors. In general, no compensation money was paid until the entire community had been relocated. Many people felt they had no choice and watched their familiar coves disappear into the distance with their hearts breaking.

In the years after the war, Canada expanded its influence, both internationally and at home. In 1945, Canada had joined the United Nations and, in 1949, had become a founding member of the North Atlantic Treaty Organisation. At home, Canada had extended its borders in 1949 with the addition of Newfoundland and Labrador as its tenth province.

The years after the war had not only encouraged the world's desire for peace and the development of human rights ideals; the end of the war left a tense division between communist and democratic countries. The start of the Cold War would begin decades of conflicts and hostility that would shape the conduct of all international relations.

*Apartment building where Igor Gouzenko lived*

# THE COLD WAR

On September 5, 1945, just after the end of World War II, a young *cipher clerk* named Igor Gouzenko, walked away from his job at the Soviet Embassy in Ottawa forever, taking with him 109 classified documents. Gouzenko approached the RCMP with his documents and stated that he wanted to defect, but they turned him away without interest. He had no luck with the newspapers that day either, and returned to his family in terror, fearing he would be found out.

Late that night, Gouzenko peered through the keyhole of his neighbor's apartment, watching as Soviet officers broke into his home across the hall and searched through his things. The next day, Gouzenko finally found someone to look at the documents he had stolen. What they revealed shattered the Western world. The Soviet Union had placed spies throughout high-ranking positions in Canada, Britain, and the United States.

Gouzenko and his family went into hiding with a new identity. In the Soviet Union, they were tried *in absentia* and

*A **cipher clerk** is a person who works at developing coded texts.*

***In absentia** means in absence.*

*Expansionism* is the policy of expanding a country's economy or territory.

*If a country is* **capitalistic**, *its economy is based on private ownership of the means of production and distribution of goods, and is characterized by a free economy.*

Igor Gouzenko

sentenced to death; their families were persecuted and imprisoned in their place. Gouzenko made several public appearances in Canada later in his life, always appearing with a white cloth over his head so his face could not be seen.

## The Iron Curtain Descends

With the information revealed in the Gouzenko documents, Canada and the rest of the Western world became very aware of the dangers facing them from the Soviet Union and its allies. Although the Soviet Union had fought together with the Allied powers during the Second World War, it had a very different ideology from the countries of North America and Western Europe. Joseph Stalin, the Soviet dictator, insisted on a tightly controlled, government-run system based on the principles of his own version of communism. The Soviet Union under Stalin also believed in aggressive *expansionism*. After the war, the majority of Eastern European countries had fallen under the Soviet influence, while Western Europe had remained democratic and *capitalistic*.

Speaking of the division between Eastern and Western Europe, Winston Churchill said that "an iron curtain has descended across the Continent." The phrase "iron curtain" came to represent the separation of communist countries from capitalist ones, a separation that resulted in the Cold War.

The Cold War was characterized by suspicion and fear, but little actual fighting (which would have made it a "Hot War"). Countries on both sides of the Iron Curtain sent spies to gather information about the activities and technological advancements of the other. People were trained to infiltrate governments and organizations for the purpose of spying.

A fear of communists and spies raged throughout Canada, as it did in the United States. People were investigated secretly and fired from sensitive positions if they were thought to be a risk. In Canada, people were often not told why they had lost their jobs, and the government frequently helped find them new jobs in positions posing less of a possible danger to national security.

The arrival of atomic weapons, introduced by the United States at the end of World War II, created a delicate balance of power during the Cold War. Atomic weapons were so powerful and did such widespread, long-lasting damage that those countries possessing nuclear technology would automatically have power over those that did not. Both the Soviet Union and the

*Sovereignty is the freedom from outside interference and the right to self-government.*

*Intercontinental ballistic missiles are self-propelled and unmanned bombs, with a range of about 3,000 to 8,000 nautical miles.*

United States had atomic weapons, and throughout the Cold War, their citizens lived in fear of a nuclear holocaust. If either country chose to use atomic weapons, the other was prepared to retaliate in kind.

Canada lay between the Soviet Union and the United States; the flight paths of bombers carrying atomic weapons would cross Canada. When the United States asked that Canada allow it to build a line of radar bases, Canadians said yes, although with some misgivings. The radar bases would warn of any Soviet bombers heading toward North America, and protect Canada as well as the United States, but some Canadians worried about letting the Americans build bases on Canadian soil. They feared they were abandoning Canada's independence and *sovereignty*.

During the 1950s, three radar lines were built across Canada. The first, the Pinetree Line, was built in 1953 and ran across southern Canada. In 1957, the Mid-Canada Line was completed, as was the Distant Early Warning (DEW) Line. The DEW Line was located north of the Arctic Circle and would provide the first information of any Soviet bomber activity. Later, when *intercontinental ballistic missiles* (ICBMs) were created, the radar stations were upgraded to provide warning in the event of a missile attack.

In 1958, Canada joined the United States to form NORAD—the North American Aerospace Defense Command. NORAD oversaw the radar lines and created plans in the case of a Soviet attack or invasion. Again, while some Canadians agreed with forming close ties with the United States, others felt Canada was simply accepting an inferior position under American control.

*ICBM launch*

# The Diefenbunker

People feared nuclear war and the destruction it would bring. As a protection against atomic weapons, many fallout shelters were built, intended to protect against the deadly radiation released by a nuclear explosion. In Canada, Prime Minister John Diefenbaker, who took office in 1957, commissioned the construction of seven large underground bunkers across the country to house politicians in case of nuclear war. The largest of these, promptly nicknamed the Diefenbunker, was located near Ottawa and would protect the prime minister and other federal politicians.

## The Korean War

At the end of World War II, the Korean Peninsula was divided in two, with North Korea becoming communist and South Korea democratic, a separation similar to that of Eastern and Western Europe. On June 25, 1950, North Korea began an invasion of South Korea. The invasion caught the Western world by surprise, but the Americans quickly called a meeting of the UN Security Council to request a UN defense of South Korea. It takes just one no vote from a permanent member of the UN Security Council to defeat a vote before it. Ordinarily, the Soviet Union—which had encouraged North Korea in their invasion plans—would have vetoed the American request, but the Soviets were boycotting the United Nations at the time. Similarly, at that time the Chinese seat on the Security Council was held not by the communist

Construction of the Diefenbunker

*Armed-forces personnel who have been **demobilized** have been discharged from service and sent home.*

People's Republic of China, but by the democratic Republic of China (Taiwan).

The first American troops, fighting under the authority of the United Nations, arrived in South Korea on July 5. Eventually, fifteen other UN members joined the Americans. Canada had **demobilized** its army after the end of World War II, as had many other countries, and Canadians took some time readying their troops. Nevertheless, by late July, four Canadian destroyers had arrived on the Pacific Coast, and a number of RCAF pilots had been sent to fight with American troops. Late in 1950, the Canadian troops began to arrive in

*Fighting during the Korean War*

Korea, and, in 1951, more Canadian soldiers joined the British Commonwealth Forces in Korea, made up of soldiers from Britain, Canada, Australia, New Zealand, and India. Eventually, over 25,000 Canadians fought in Korea; 516 were killed.

By late September of 1950, the North Koreans had been pushed out of South Korea, which they had rapidly conquered in late June. Instead of ending the fighting at that point, the Americans decided to keep going and try to unite all of Korea under a democratic government. When the UN forces began to push into North Korea, the Chinese sent troops to help the North Koreans. In later years, Russia revealed that the Soviet Union had supported North Korea in the war, but had not wanted to face

*The Chinese Field Army moved great numbers of battle-hardened veterans into North Korea.*

71

*A **demilitarized zone** is an officially recognized area from which all military personnel, weapons, and installations have been removed following an agreement to stop fighting.*

the Americans directly. Instead, they encouraged the Chinese to attack.

With the entry of the Chinese, the two sides were much more evenly matched. The war dragged on for nearly another two years before a cease-fire was declared to end the stalemate on July 27, 1953. No peace treaty was ever signed between North and South Korea; instead, a **demilitarized zone** was set up between the two countries, with armed troops constantly patrolling both sides of the zone.

The Korean War grew out of Cold War tensions between the communist and democratic countries. North Korea, along with China and the Soviet Union, who had encouraged the invasion, had thought taking over the southern half of the Korean Peninsula would be quick and easy. The war was the first international conflict of the Cold War—but it would not be the last.

## The Suez Crisis

Three years after the end of the Korean War, another international crisis took place. The war over the Suez Canal in Egypt, linking the Red Sea with the Mediterranean Sea, was very different from the Korean War and initially involved neither the Soviet Union nor the United States. Still, the Cold War

*The Suez Canal*

*To be a **nationalist** is to have a proud loyalty and devotion to a nation.*

affected the Suez crisis, as it affected nearly all international relations at that time.

The Suez Canal had been under the control of Britain and France until July of 1956, when the ***nationalist*** government of Egyptian president Gamal Abdel Nasser put it under Egyptian control, preventing Israeli ships from using it. Israel was allied with both Britain and France, and none of the three were happy about Nasser's actions. Israel wanted to be able

*The organization of UNEF was created to help bring about a peaceful resolution to the Suez crisis.*

*Canadian armed forces*

to use the Suez, while Britain and France wanted the enormous profits canal traffic generated transporting oil from the Persian Gulf to Europe.

Britain, France, and Israel met secretly and formed a plan to regain control of the Suez. First, Israel would invade the Sinai Peninsula and clash with Egyptian troops.

*A 1956 political cartoon portrays Nassar's mixed messages to the Western world.*

Then, British and French forces would arrive to stop the fighting and would retake control of the canal in the process.

On October 29, 1956, Israel invaded the Sinai Peninsula. When Britain and France offered to settle the dispute and occupy the area between Israel and Egypt, Nasser refused. Consequently, Britain and France began attacks against Egypt on October 31 to try to regain control of the canal.

Although British, French, and Israeli forces quickly succeeded in capturing the

Sinai Peninsula and the Suez Canal, the war was very unpopular with the rest of the world. The Soviet Union threatened to intervene on behalf of Egypt and begin bombing London and Paris. The United States, fearing the conflict could quickly escalate into a third world war, pressured Britain and France into pulling out of the area early in 1957. By that time, however, the Suez Canal had been recaptured, the goal of the operation.

Canada had refused to support Britain during the attack on Egypt. When Britain had asked for Canadian help, Prime Minister St. Laurent responded that Canada owed its allegiance to the United Nations, not to Britain. During the worst of the crisis, Lester Bowles Pearson, acting cabinet minister of external affairs in Canada, had gone to the United Nations with a proposal. Pearson recommended a United Nations Emergency Force (UNEF) be created to patrol the borders while working out a peaceful solution to the situation. This led to the creation of the UN Peacekeeping Force, for which Pearson was awarded the Nobel Peace Prize in 1957.

The previous three decades had been tumultuous for Canada and for the world. The 1930s had brought the Great Depression and severe economic hardships to millions of Canadians. The 1940s had brought another world war; with the end of the Second World War, a Cold War began that would shape much of the remaining twentieth century.

The 1960s would ignite a social awakening in Canada. People would become very aware of environmental issues, springing from an increased reliance on oil and the beginning of nuclear power. In Québec, French Canadians would seek to develop a Québécois national identity, unique from the larger Canadian identity. This new social awareness would lead to a restructuring of what it meant to be Canadian.

1935 The "Royal Twenty-Centers" go on strike and embark on the On-to-Ottawa Trek.

September 1, 1939 Germans attack Wielun, Poland.

October 24, 1929 Black Thursday leads to the Great Depression.

June 25, 1940 France surrenders to Germany.

July 28, 1930 R. B. Bennett and the Conservative Party win Canadian general election.

September 10, 1939 Canada enters World War II.

July 1940 The air war begins and will last until May 1941.

May 1942 U-boat attacks begin in Canadian waters.

April 1941 Canada begins drafting men under the National Resources Mobilization Act.

December 7, 1941 Japan bombs Pearl Harbor, Hawaii.

June 6, 1944 The D-Day attack begins in France.

November 1941 Canada sends troops to Hong Kong to help protect it against Japan.

December 8, 1941 Japan attacks Hong Kong.

December 25, 1941 Hong Kong surrenders to Japan.

October 14, 1942 S.S. *Caribou* is attacked, and more than one hundred die.

1945 Canada joins the United Nations.

1949 Canada joins NATO.

May 7, 1945 Germany surrenders to the Allies.

March 31, 1949 Newfoundland and Labrador become Canada's tenth province.

June 26, 1945 The United Nations is established.

April 4, 1949 NATO is established.

September 5, 1945 The Igor Gouzenko affair begins with his defection.

December 10, 1948 The United Nations adopts the Universal Declaration of Human Rights.

80

**July 27, 1953 Korean conflict reaches a cease-fire.**

**1958 Canada joins the North American Aerospace Defense Command.**

**1988 Canadian government offers apology to Japanese who had been placed in internment camps.**

**1950 Resettlement plan begins in Newfoundland and Labrador.**

**1950s Radar lines are built across Canada.**

**1957 Lester Bowles Pearson wins the Nobel Peace Prize for establishing the UN Peacekeeping Force.**

**1950 Canadian troops arrive in Korea.**

**1982 Canada adopts the Charter of Rights and Freedoms.**

## FURTHER READING

Baker, David. *William Avery "Billy" Bishop: The Man and the Aircraft He Flew*. Los Angeles: Books Nippan, 1991.

Benham, Mary Lile. *Nellie McClung*. Markham, Ont.: Fitzhenry & Whiteside, 2000.

Bumstead, J. M. *Winnipeg General Strike of 1919: An Illustrated History*. Winnipeg, Man.: J. Gordon Shillingford Publishing, 1996.

Fraser, Donald. *The Journal of Private Fraser: Canadian Expeditionary Force, 1914–1918*. Ottawa, Ont.: CEF Books, 2002.

Glasner, Joyce. *The Halifax Explosion: Surviving the Blast that Shook a Nation*. Canmore, Alb.: Altitude Publishing, 2003.

Millar, Nancy. *The Famous Five: Five Canadian Women and Their Fight to Become Persons*. Calgary, Alb.: Deadwood Publishing, 2003.

Ostrower, Gary B. *League of Nations 1919*. Wayne, N.J.: Avery Publishing Group, 1996.

Robson, Pam. *All About the First World War, 1914–18*. London: Hodder Wayland, 2003.

Spigelman, Martin. *Wilfrid Laurier*. Markham, Ont.: Fitzhenry & Whiteside, 2000.

Turner, I. A. J. *Vimy Ridge, 1917: Byng's Canadians Triumph at Arras*. University Park, Ill.: Osprey Publishing, 2005.

## FOR MORE INFORMATION

Canada and the First World War
www.collectionscanada.ca/firstworldwar/
index-e.html

Canadian Labor History
www.civilization.ca/hist/labour/
lab01e.html

The Famous Five
www.collectionscanada.ca/famous5/
index-e.html

Imperial Adventure: Canada
and the Boer War
www.civilization.ca/cwm/saw/
index_e.html

In Flanders Fields Museum
www.inflandersfields.be/default2.htm

Newfoundland and the Great War
collections.ic.gc.ca/great_war/home.html

Sir Robert Laird Borden
www.collectionscanada.ca/
primeministers/h4-3200-e.html

Sir Wilfrid Laurier
www.collectionscanada.ca/
primeministers/h4-3175-e.html

The Suffrage Movement
timelinks.merlin.mb.ca/referenc/
db0007.htm

Veteran's Affairs Canada:
The First World War
www.vacacc.gc.ca/general/
sub.cfm?source=history/firstwar

# INDEX

## PICTURE CREDITS

## BIOGRAPHIES

Sheila Nelson was born in Newfoundland and grew up in both Newfoundland and Ontario. She has written a number of history books for kids and always enjoys the chance to keep learning. She recently earned a master's degree and now lives in Rochester, New York, with her husband and daughter.

## SERIES CONSULTANT

Dr. David Bercuson is the Director of the Centre for Military and Strategic Studies at the University of Calgary. His writings on modern Canadian politics, Canadian defense and foreign policy, and Canadian military, among other topics, have appeared in academic and popular publications. Dr. Bercuson is the author, coauthor, or editor of more than thirty books, including *Confrontation at Winnipeg: Labour, Industrial Relations, and the General Strike* (1990), *Colonies: Canada to 1867* (1992), *Maple Leaf Against the Axis, Canada's Second World War* (1995), and *Christmas in Washington: Roosevelt and Churchill Forge the Alliance* (2005). He has also served as historical consultant for several film and television projects, and provided political commentary for CBC radio and television and CTV television. In 1989, Dr. Bercuson was elected a fellow of the Royal Society of Canada. In 2004, Dr. Bercuson received the Vimy Award, sponsored by the Conference of Defence Association Institute, in recognition of his significant contributions to Canada's defense and the preservation of the Canadian democratic principles.